THIS WALKER BOOK BELONGS TO:

_____

_____

_____

_____

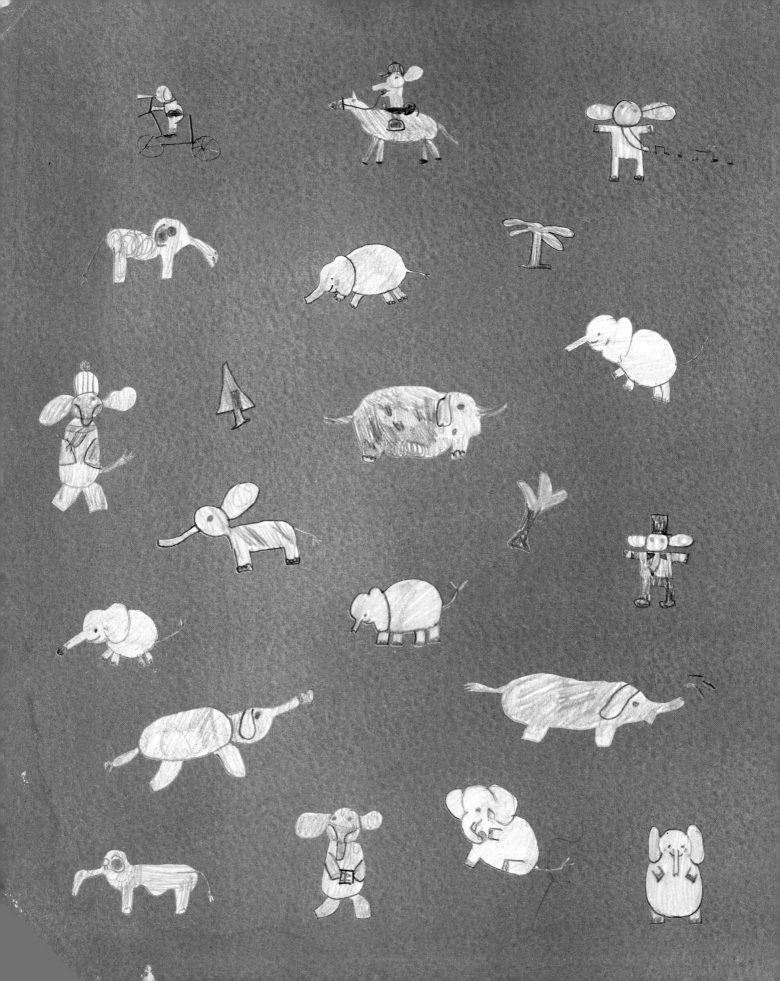

For Bryan and Sarah

with thanks to
Melissa Appleton, Sarah and Rowan Dale
for the elephant endpapers, and David Lloyd
for seeing the wood.

First published 1991
by Walker Books Ltd, 87 Vauxhall Walk
London SE11 5HJ

This edition published 1999

2 4 6 8 10 9 7 5 3 1

© 1991 Penny Dale

Printed in Hong Kong/China

British Library Cataloguing in Publication Data
A catalogue record for this book is
available from the British Library.

ISBN 0-7445-6954-0

The Elephant Tree

Penny Dale

WALKER BOOKS
AND SUBSIDIARIES
LONDON • BOSTON • SYDNEY

Elephant wanted to climb a tree.

So we went to find the elephant tree.

We walked and we walked.

We looked and we looked.

"Is this the elephant tree?"
"No," said the birds.
"It's the bird tree."

"Is this the elephant tree?"

"No," said the monkeys.
"It's the monkey tree."

"Is this the elephant tree?"
"No," said the tigers.
"It's the tiger tree."

"Are any of these the elephant tree?"

"No," said the bears.

"These are bear trees."

We ran and we ran.

We walked and we walked.

We looked and we looked.

But we still couldn't find the elephant tree.

Never mind, Elephant.

Wait and see.

Here it is. Look.

The elephant tree.

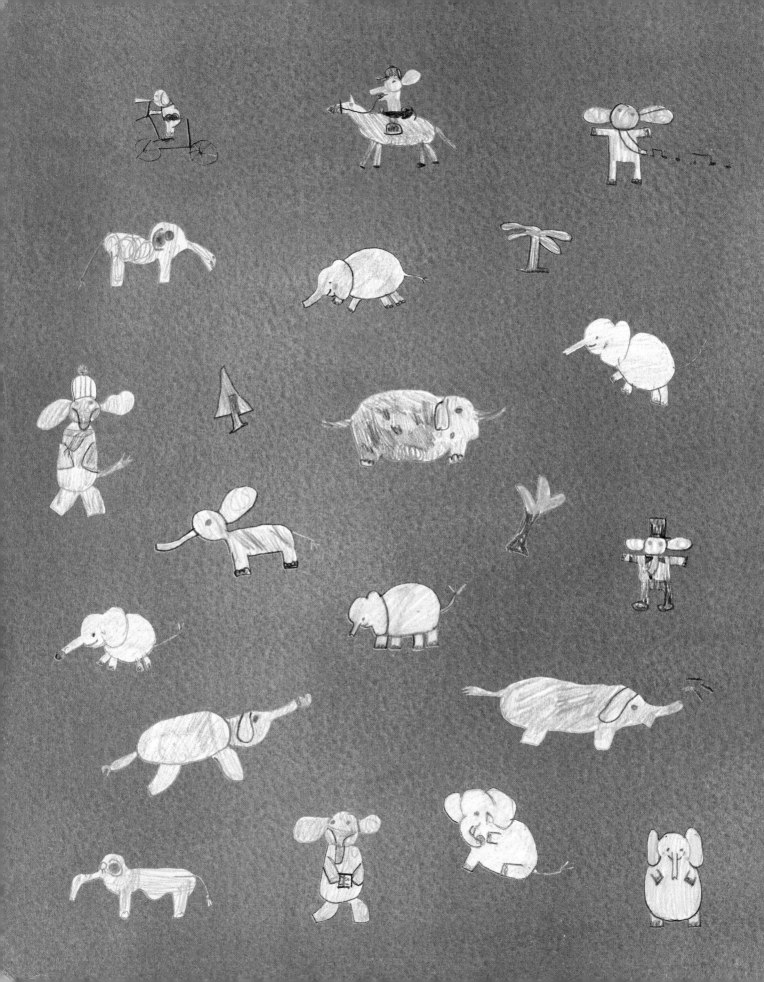

MORE WALKER PAPERBACKS
For You to Enjoy

Also by Penny Dale

TEN IN THE BED

"A subtle variation on the traditional nursery song, illustrated with wonderfully warm pictures … crammed with amusing details."
Practical Parenting

0-7445-1340-5   £4.99

TEN OUT OF BED

"A counting backwards version of 'Ten in the Bed'…
Penny Dale's warm and distinctive illustrations are full of action and movement …
lots to look at, smile at and talk about." *Children's Books of the Year*

0-7445-4383-5   £4.99

BIG BROTHER, LITTLE BROTHER

When Little Brother cries and points and shouts,
Big Brother knows why. He makes Little Brother happy.
But the course of brotherly love does not always run smooth –
and when Big Brother cries, what will Little Brother do?

"Penny Dale's beautiful drawings sensitively show the ups and downs
of the affectionate relationship between the two brothers."
Practical Parenting

0-7445-6953-2   £4.99